REALLY RAPT

Compiled by
Susan Hill

Era

Published by Era Publications,
220 Grange Road, Flinders Park, SA 5025 Australia

Text © Susan Hill, 1990
Illustration by Steven Woolman
Cover design by Quang Bui
Printed in Hong Kong
First published 1991

National Library of Australia
Cataloguing-in-Publication Data:

    Really rapt.

    ISBN 1 86374 001 5 (Pbk.).

    1. Readers (Primary). 2. Nursery rhymes.
    I. Hill, Susan, 1946-    . II. Title

428.6

For worldwide distribution details of
this book see Era Publications' website:
## http://www.era-publications.com.au

**Acknowledgements**
**Yellow Butter**, from *Yellow Butter, Purple Jelly, Red Jam, Black Bread*
(1981) Viking Press, N.Y., reprinted by permission of Gina Maccoby Literary Agency, © 1981, Mary Hoberman. **My Mother Says I'm Sickening**, and
**I Do Not like the Rat**, from *The New Kid on the Block*, Wm. Heinemann
Ltd, reprinted by permission of Octopus Publishing Group Library, U.K. and
Wm Morrow and Co. Inc/Publishers, N.Y., U.S.A. **Wobbly Wheel**, from *Smile
Please!* (1987) Viking Kestrel, © Tony Bradman, 1987, reproduced by
permission of Penguin Books Ltd. **Head and Shoulders, Baby** reprinted by
permission of Warner/Chappell Music, and © Essex Music of Australia Pty
Ltd. **Oodles of Noodles**, L. & J. Hymes Jnr, © 1964 by Addison Wesley
Pub. Co Inc., Reading, MA, U.S.A. **Garbage Delight**, © Dennis Lee, from
*Garbage Delight* by Dennis Lee, Published by Macmillan of Canada.

The publisher has made all efforts to trace material used in this book. If
any has been used without recognition, the author and publisher offer
unreserved apology.

15   14   13   12   11   10   9   8   7   6

# Contents

# Introduction

Many of these raps, chants, rhymes and clapping games can be heard on street corners and in playgrounds. Some are poems that work well when read aloud. Use the suggestions for reading aloud but, remember, the best arrangements are ones you make yourself.

The words in the chants or raps are often spoken with a steady 4/4 beat. Feel the rhythm. Foot stamps and hand claps help you keep the beat at a steady pace.

## Improvization techniques

### Voice, volume, pace and expression

Use a lead voice for one line and a group voice for the next line. Build up voices, adding one reader at a time. Start out slowly and pick up the pace. Vary from soft to loud. Try different expressions — excited and happy, mean and angry, sad and sorrowful or proud and arrogant.

## *Claps, clicks, hand jives and foot stamps*

In some words there is a stress or emphasis. Stamp your feet, click fingers, clap or hand jive on these words. A hand jive is a quick sequence of slapping sounds — on your thigh, the back of your hand, the front of your hand and on your chest or arm. Use different sounds, sharp and light then deep and low, to keep the rhythm.

You can combine clicks (∗), claps (+) and stamps in various ways like this:

| **Lead voice** | **Group voice** |
| --- | --- |
| The other day, | The other day, |
| I met a bear, | I met a bear, |
| In groovy shoes, | In groovy shoes, |
| A smacking good pair. | A smacking good pair. |

(Repeat without the group voice and add foot stamps.)

Rehearse and perform the raps, chants and rhymes and keep the fun alive!

# My Mama Told Me

My mama told me,
If I was goody,
That she would buy me
A rubber **dolly**

My aunty told her,
I kissed a soldier,
Now she won't buy me
A rubber **dolly**

Traditional

T    Clap thighs.
O    Clap own hands.
L    Clap left hands.
R    Clap right hands.

(The pattern goes T O R  T O L  and repeat.)

# Three - Six - Nine

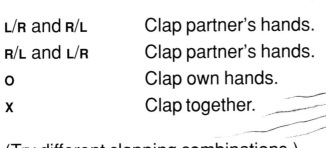

Three - six - nine,
The goose drank wine,
The monkey chewed tobacco,
On the street car line.
The line broke,
The monkey got choked,
And they all went to heaven
In a little rubber boat.

Clap, clap.

Anonymous

| | |
|---|---|
| L/R and R/L | Clap partner's hands. |
| R/L and L/R | Clap partner's hands. |
| o | Clap own hands. |
| x | Clap together. |

(Try different clapping combinations.)

# Miss Mary Mac, Mac, Mac

Miss Mary Mac, Mac, Mac,
All dressed in **black, black, black,**
With silver buttons, buttons,
    buttons,
All down her back, back, back.

Miss Betty Bean, Bean, Bean,
All dressed in *green, green,*
    *green.*
She never smiled, smiled, smiled,
She was too mean, mean, mean.

Miss Lucy Light, Light, Light,
All dressed in **white, white, white.**
She tricked her brother, brother,
    brother,
Just out of spite, spite, spite.

There's soda crackers, crackers,
  crackers,
Up on the shelf, shelf, shelf.
If you want any more, more, more,
You can sing it yourself, self, **self**.

Anonymous

Miss  Ma - ry   Mac   Mac   Mac  All Dressed in ...
  O    R   O    L   O   R   O   X   O    R    O...

o   Clap own hands.
R   Clap right hands.
L   Clap left hands.
x   Clap partner's hands.

# Bears in Groovy Shoes

Lead voice:  **Group voice:**

The o*ther da*y,  ***The o+ther da+y,***
I me*t a be*ar,  ***I me+t a bea+r,***
In gro*ovy shoe*s  ***In gro+ovy shoe+s,***
A sma*cking  ***A sma+cking***
    good pa*ir.      ***good pa+ir.***

(Repeat without the echo.)


He looked at me,
I looked at him,
He stared at me,      ***(Echo)***
I stared at him.

(Repeat without the echo.)

He said to me,
"Why don't you run?
I see you have
N't any gun."

And so I ran
Away from there,
But right behind
Me was that bear.

Ahead of me
There was a tree,
A great big tree
Ahead of me.

And so I jumped
Into the air,
But I missed that branch
Away up there

Now don't you fret,
Now don't you frown,
'Cos I caught that branch
On the way back down.

The moral of
This story is

**All:**

Don't talk to bears in groovy shoes

Anonymous

# Yellow Butter

1: Yellow butter, purple jelly, red
jam, black bread.

2: Spread it thick,

3: Say it quick,

1: Yellow butter, purple jelly, red
jam, black bread.

2: Spread it thicker,

3: Say it quicker,

1: Yellow butter, purple jelly, red
jam, black bread.

2: Now repeat it,

3: While you eat it,

1: Yellow butter, purple jelly, red
jam, black bread.

**All:**
*Don't talk with your
mouth full!*

Mary Ann Hoberman

# Chicken and Chips

1:    Chicken and chips,

2:    Chicken and chips,

**All:**  ***Everybody here likes chicken and chips.***

1:    We eat them all day,

2:    Never throw them away,

**All:**  ***We all like chicken and chips.***

1:    Choc ice and chips,

2:    Choc ice and chips,

**All:**  ***Everyone here likes choc ice and chips.***

1:    We eat them all day,

2:    Never throw them away,

**All:**  ***We all like choc ice and chips.***

(Sit in circles. Clap own hands then clap hands with people next to you.)

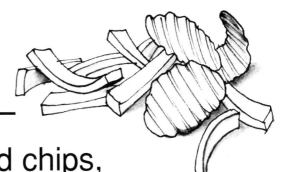

1: Chop suey and chips,

2: Chop suey and chips,

**All: *Everyone here likes chop suey and chips.***

1: We eat them all day,

2: Never throw them away,

**All: *We all like chop suey and chips.***

1: Chips and chips,

2: Chips and chips,

**All: *Everyone here likes chips and chips.***

1: We eat them all day,

2: Never throw them away,

**All: *We all like chips and chips.***

Anonymous

# The Goat

(Click at ★)

1:    There was a man, ★ ★

2:    Now please take note, ★ ★

1:    There was a man, ★ ★

2:    Who had a goat, ★ ★

1:    He loved that goat, ★ ★

2:    Indeed he did, ★ ★

**All:** ***He loved that goat,***
***Just like a kid.***

1:    One day that goat

2:    Felt frisky and fine,

1:    Ate three red shirts

2:    From off the line.

1:    The man he grabbed

2:    Him by the back,

**All:** ***And tied him to***
***A railroad track.***

1:     But when the train

2:     Came into sight,

1:     That goat grew pale

2:     And green with fright.

1:     He heaved a sigh,

2:     As if in pain,

**All:**  *Coughed up those shirts*
*And flagged the train.*

Anonymous

(Divide in 3 groups. One group makes steam-train sounds at the smoke puffs.)

# My Mother Says I'm Sickening

1: My mother says I'm sickening,
   My mother says I'm crude.
   She says this when she sees
      me
   Playing ping pong with my
      food.
   She doesn't seem to like it
   When I slurp my bowl of stew,
   And now she's got a list of
      things
   She says I musn't do —

2: Do not catapult the carrots!
3: Do not juggle gobs of fat!
4: Do not drop the mashed
      potatoes
5: On the gerbil or the cat!

6: Never punch the pumpkin
    pudding!
7: Never tunnel through the bread!
8: Put no peas into your pocket!
9: Place no noodles on your head!
10: Do not squeeze the steamed
    zucchini!
11: Do not make the melon ooze!
12: Never stuff vanilla yoghurt
13: In your little sister's shoes!
14: Draw no faces in the ketchup!
15: Make no little gravy pools!

1: I wish my mother wouldn't make
    so many useless rules.

Jack Prelutsky

(Read it softly and angrily, getting louder and angrier.)

# Little Miss Muffet

( on the beat )

Little Miss Muffet
Sat on a tuffet,
Eating her curds and whey.
Along came a spider,
Who sat down beside her
And said, "Is this seat taken?"

Little Miss Muffet
Sat on a tuffet,
Eating her Irish stew.
Along came a spider,
Who sat down beside her,
So she ate the spider up, too.

Little Miss . . .
Sat on a . . .
Eating her . . .
Along came . . .
Who . . .

. . .

your turn

Anonymous

# I Left My Ma in New Orleans

I left my Ma in New Orleans,
With forty-five cents
And a can of beans,
'Cause I thought it was right, right,
Right for my country.
Whoops - i - do!
Left, left,
I left my Ma in New Orleans,

(Repeat from first line.)

Traditional

(This is a foot-stamping, marching song. When reading 'whoops-i-do', jump up and land on your left foot. Repeat.)

# The Wobbly Wheel

1:      This is the story

2:      Of my friend Neil,

1:      Who had a bike

2:      With a wobbly wheel.

1:      A wobbly wheel —

2:      A wobbly wheel —

1:      Oh, whoops!

**All:   *And there it goes.***

| | |
|---|---|
| 1: | Neil went racing |
| 2: | Down the street, |
| 1: | Pedalling fast |
| 2: | With both his feet. |
| 1: | Both his feet — |
| 2: | Both his feet — |
| 1: | Oh, whoops! |
| **All:** | ***And there they go.*** |

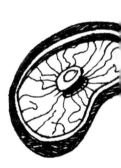

| | |
|---|---|
| 1: | The wobbly wheel |
| 2: | Went round and round. |
| 1: | When it flew off, |
| 2: | Neil hit the ground. |
| 1: | Hit the ground — |
| 2: | Hit the ground — |
| 1: | Oh, whoops! |
| **All:** | ***And there he goes.*** |

1:    Then Neil got up
2:    And with a groan,
1:    He rubbed his head
2:    And walked off home.
1:    Walked off home —
2:    Walked off home —
1:    Oh, wh<sup>o</sup>op<sub></sub>s!
**All:    *And there he goes.***

1:    Neil had a bump
2:    That he could feel,
1:    So he sold his bike
2:    With that wobbly wheel.
1:    That wobbly wheel —
2:    That wobbly wheel —
1:    Oh, whoops!
**All:    *And there it goes.***

Tony Bradman

# I Do Not Like the Rat!

1:  I praise the hippopotamus,

2:  I celebrate the bat,

3:  I hold the bream in high esteem,

**All:**

   **BUT I DO NOT LIKE THE RAT!**

1:  I cotton to the octopus,

2:  I tolerate the gnat,

3:  I dote upon the stately swan —

**All:**

   **I *SHUDDER* AT THE RAT!**

1:  I value the rhinoceros,

2:  I venerate the cat,

3:  I quite salute the simple newt —

**All:**

   **I CANNOT *STAND THE RAT!***

Jack Prelutsky

# Head and Shoulders, Baby

Head and shoulders, baby,

ʀ One,

ʀx Two,

ʀ Three.

Head and shoulders, baby,

ʟ One,

ʟx Two,

ʟ Three.

Head and shoulders,

Head and shoulders,

Head and shoulders, baby,

ʀ One,

ʀx Two,

ʀ Three.

**Hand Jive**

| | |
|---|---|
| L | Slap left thigh with left hand. |
| LX | Lift hand and slap top of left hand with right hand. |
| R | Slap right thigh with right hand. |
| RX | Lift hand and slap top of right hand with left hand. |

Knee and ankle, baby,
One, two, three.
Knee and ankle, baby,
One, two, three.
Knee and ankle,
Knee and ankle,
Knee and ankle, baby,
One, two, three.

Milk the cow, baby,
One, two, three.
Milk the cow, baby,
One, two, three.
Milk the cow,
Milk the cow,
Milk the cow, baby,
One, two, three.

Throw the ball, baby,
One, two, three.
Throw the ball, baby,
One, two, three.
Throw the ball,
Throw the ball,
Throw the ball, baby,
One, two, three.

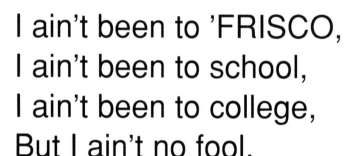

I ain't been to 'FRISCO,
I ain't been to school,
I ain't been to college,
But I ain't no fool.
To the front . . .         (Jump to the front)
To the back . . .         (Jump back)
To the front . . .
To the back . . .
To the si- si- side . . .      (Jump left)
To the si- si- side . . .      (Jump right)

Bessie Jones

# Oodles of Noodles

 I love noodles. Give me oodles.
 Make a mound up to the sun.
 Noodles are my favorite foodles.
 I eat noodles by the ton.

Lucia and James L. Hymes, Jnr.

(This is a round.
Actions can be performed at each line.)

# Garbage Delight

Now, I'm not the one
To say, "No," to a bun,
And I always can manage
    some jelly;
If somebody gurgles,
"Please eat my hamburgles,"
I try to make room in my belly.
I seem, if they scream,
Not to gag on ice-cream
And with fudge I can choke
    down my fright;
But none is enticing
Or even worth slicing,
Compared with
**Garbage Delight.**

With a nip and a nibble,
A drip and a dribble,
A dollop, a walloping bite;
If you want to see grins
All the way to my shins,
Then give me some
**Garbage Delight!**

I'm handy with candy,
I star with a bar,
And I'm known for my butter-
    scotch burp;
I can stare in the eyes
Of a Toffee Surprise
And polish it off with one slurp.
My lick is the longest,

My chomp is the champ,
And everyone envies my bite;
But my talents were wasted,
Until I had tasted
The wonders of
**Garbage Delight.**

With a nip and a nibble,
A drip and a dribble,
A dollop, a walloping bite;
If you want to see grins
All the way to my shins,
Then give me some
Garbage Delight, right now!
Please pass me some
**Garbage Delight!**

Dennis Lee